How To Balance Coaching With School

Along with How to Remember Things Faster & Score Marks

Hrishikesh Goswami

pencil

ISBN 978-93-5667-460-8
© Hrishikesh Goswami 2023
Published in India 2023 by Pencil

A brand of
One Point Six Technologies Pvt. Ltd.
123, Building J2, Shram Seva Premises,
Wadala Truck Terminal, Wadala (E)
Mumbai 400037, Maharashtra, INDIA
E connect@thepencilapp.com
W www.thepencilapp.com

DISCLAIMER: *The opinions expressed in this book are those of the authors and do not purport to reflect the views of the Publisher.*

Author biography

(India Book of Records Holder for Poetry) (Creative Endeavour of The Month April 2021 by The Assam Tribune) (Recipient of India Prime Top 100 Author Award 2022) (Recipient of India Star Icon Award 2022)(Author of The Year 2021 Nominee) (Recipient of The Leading Attainers Award 2022) HRISHIKESH GOSWAMI is a Contemporary Naturalistic poet from Assam, India who specialises in writing about nature and realism coalescing fiction and non -fiction in a sophisticated blend. Author of The Poet's Words, The Secret: Nature Reveals, Poems for Poets, The Exegesis, 72 Haiku, 51st Tanka, The Sesquipedalian Notion, An Aureate Opus of Quotes, An Ode To, The Arcane: The Adventures in Lavender, The Arcane: The Ultimate Fate, A Poet's Whim For Serendipity, A Fortuitous Odyssey, The Adventures of James Tony Morgan along with Co-Author of World Record Anthology Book – "Bilingual Aesthetics" and editor of the E-Poetry Anthology 'The Euphoric Verses from Soul' and the Literary Anthology 'Forest & Me' and 'The Idiosyncratic Mystery'. Hrishikesh Goswami fell in love with writing from a fledgling age of 14 when he was at the 9th standard. Hrishikesh Goswami's poems have been featured in The Assam Tribune, Blue Lake Review, Indian Poetry Review, the Weaver Magazine, Poets India, Soul Connection brought up by Guwahati Grand Poetry Festival, Anthology Still I Rise brought out by Wingless Dreamer, Winter Poems Anthology brought out by Poets Choice. Hrishikesh Goswami has been highlighted by Media Houses such as India Saga, Daily hunt, Spot Latest, Fox Story India, Glamwist etc. Hrishikesh Goswami is also available in E platforms like Story mirror, Anchor, Spotify, Wattpad, Google Podcast, Apple Podcast, Breaker, Pocket Cast, Radio Public, All Poetry, Listen Notes, Wynk Music, Poetry Soup, Commaful, Hello Poetry, SoundCloud, Poem Hunter, Scribd, Vivlio, Angus & Robertson Store, Mondadori Store, Thalia, Indigo Books & Music, Kobo Inc., Apple Books etc. for his dear readers. Readers can find further information about the poet in Google and

YouTube by typing "POET HRISHIKESH GOSWAMI "
for the same.

Hrishikesh Goswami has cracked several competitive
exams such as JEE Mains 2022, NEET-UG 2022, CUET
2022, IISER IAT 2022, KVPY 2022, AAU CET 2022,
ASTU CEE 2022, IOQB-I and IOQC-I. He has been
bestowed with Certificate of Commendation in Never
Such Innocence International Poetry Contest, Certificate
of Achievement from Asian Council for English
Proficiency Test conducted under CAFLR norms,
Certificate of Merit for Outstanding Performance in
NationWide Mega Science Experiment Conducted by
NCERT, VVM, VIBHA and Ministry of Education, Govt.
of India, Editor's Choice Award in International Essay
Writing Competition by Monomousumi and is recognised
by World Record University, Career Development College
London, Guwahati Grand Poetry Festival, WWF India,
APJ. Abdul Kalam International Foundation, ASSIST
WORLD RECORDS, PONDICHERRY BOOK OF
RECORDS and Royal Commonwealth Society. He has
been two times State Level Tae-kwon-do Champion, Gold
Medallist of several National and International
Competitive Exams and Olympiads, a KVPY Scholar,
Winner of National School Level Essay Writing Contest
conducted by Maulana Abul Kalam Azad Awards 2020,
Grand Master of Mental Arithmetic-Senior A Whole Brain
Development Program from Aloha (Abacus), Visharat in
Hindustani Classical Music, Best Debater of PRARAMBH
2021 conducted by Nehru Group of Institutions, Kerala
and Holder of Honourable Mention in several notable
Poetry Competitions from around the World.

Apart from these Hrishikesh's poems have been critically analysed by Fruit Journal Manchester (UK), Acorn (A journal of contemporary haiku), The Leading Edge Magazine, BreakBread Magazine and has been published by The Assam Tribune's Horizon and Planet Young, NEZINE (An online magazine), Noverse Foundation and FoxGales Publishers, Poem hunter-The World's Poetry Archive, Cultural Reverence (An International Digital Journal Of Art and Literature), Tech Touch Talk of Kolkata.

Hrishikesh Goswami's poems have been read by The Liminal Review, Poetry London, Appalachian Review, The Tether's End, Tears in the Fence Literary Journal, MASKS Literary Magazine, Ribbons, The Hopper (An environmental literary magazine), The West Trade Review, Split Rock Review, The Baltimore Review, Rollick Magazine, The Poetry Magazine, Chestnut Review, The Sun Magazine, The Society of Classical Poets, The Greensboro Review, The London Magazine, The Kenyon Review, The Adroit Journal, Washington Square Review, Wilderness House Literary Review and many more. Hrishikesh's haiku poem has been translated into Japanese and published in a traditional Japanese style literary anthology.

Nevertheless Hrishikesh's poems have been able to gratify the minds of critics to an extent and hopes to improve this range in the upcoming years. A few of his poems have also been widely accepted in Poetry Circles and Forums.

CONTENTS

Salient Features of this Manuscript 10

How to Use This Book 12

What is the Aim of this Manuscript 13

How to Save Time 14

How to Remember Things Faster 18

How To Retain Things Effectively 20

Importance of Knowledge 23

How To Score Marks 25

How To Balance Coaching With School 29

How To Analyse Results 34

Importance of Improving Oneself 36

Preface

The only thing I would say is that now that you have picked up this book please read it completely. If you can't finish it in one go, no issues! Take your time and read because a book half understood can prove to be very unsafe! I have experienced it myself. If you get stuck or find any trouble in correlating the things given here with your daily life, I suggest you halt the reading process for a short time span and just relax. If you are having exams, finish them first and then read this book with full dedication. You will surely enjoy it!

Acknowledgements

I hereby would like to acknowledge my father Dr. Anjan Goswami and my mother Mrs. Pallabi Goswami for always standing by my side when I required them the most!

I also would take the time to thank my teachers and professors for helping me out in each and every aspect of life. Their philosophies and opinions inspire me to meditate and understand complex entities from a different perspective!

Lastly, my heartfelt thanks to my readers for opting this book from the huge assembly of books. Although I don't know the exact reason behind your choice, I can make some wild guesses!

Salient Features of this Manuscript

1.   Before unveiling the salient features, I want you to close your eyes for at least a minute in deep silence and think about the good things in your life.

Are you done? If yes, you can proceed further…

2.   This book is written keeping in mind the common obstacles offered by a variety of circumstances encountered by people, especially students preparing for certain examinations. There is a gargantuan amount of hassle, especially on students who need to manage coaching classes alongside their regular school schedule.

3.   This book contains effective ways of handling pressure and stress.

4.   The book focuses not only on academic aspects but also on the allied fields.

5.   Students can read the book in their free time as and when they feel like reading.

6.   This is a self-help book and aims solely at the emotional and academic upliftment of the readers!

7.   This book is not 'bulky'!

8.   Readers have the choice to decide how they want to read! (*However reading in the given sequence is recommended.*)

9.   The book is very portable and can be carried anywhere. It shall not act as a liability to its purchaser.

10.   Unnecessary stories are omitted to keep things simple and concise.

How to Use This Book

I don't want to tell you how to read a book, for you will definitely know that…it's very simple! I just want to ensure that what you will be reading in the subsequent chapters should help you achieve a better version of yourself! That is my ambition as well as that of this book in your hands. Students have to face diverse kinds of hassles and the best way to deal with them is by facing them with a *'stronger you'*! Accept this book as your best *workmate* and read it in your free time to make good use of that time and at the same time improve your performance as a student! The gigantic amount of workload on students is a very common problem and one should know the means of tackling them. This book will be successful only if it is able to make you one (*stronger you*)!

What is the Aim of this Manuscript

The one and only purpose of this manuscript is to diminish the stress, anxiety and pressure on students who are expected to simultaneously cope up with both coaching and school by providing them with helpful tricks and tips! The book also wants to make the students valiant in facing the academic problems and help them in handling pressure.

The concepts taught in schools and coaching institutions should not confuse the students and this is what the aim of this book is! There are many ways of overpowering pressure but which way is the best for you can only be decided by you and no one else. But to be in a position to decide, you must know all the ways...which sounds very obvious, isn't it?

How to Save Time

You will find a lot of articles on how to save time, won't you? In fact I have written a couple of articles taking *time*as the main objective! But there is a buried issue in reading these articles which I am sure most of you are not well aware of! Articles motivate us but only for a short period of time, whereas a book keeps us motivated throughout the reading period plus the extra time which differs from person to person. One who reads a book superficially forgets the title of the book maybe within hours after reading but one who is totally devoted to reading will not forget the key message of the book till death!!

For students time is very vital. Wasting a single second can be very detrimental because time as we know never puts reverse gear! Students mainly lose their time in travelling (say you need half an hour to reach home from school or you need forty five minutes from your home to your respective coaching centre).These fragments of time when summed up at the end of the month will show you something extraordinary! Try it yourself for this month!

Apart from travelling time is also unexploited in chatting unwanted or insignificant stuff with your friends. This is also a key factor for generating distractions. The time you spend with your friend is valuable only if you come out with something productive at the end of the discussion. Say for instance you are supposed to decide a venue for an important meeting with your friends. You need a venue that is suitable for all. So you decide to consult your friends over the conference call and deliberate about the venue for about an hour and then one of your friends pops up and declares that he will not be able to go to that place for certain reasons. Then you all again have to start from scratch resulting in the loss of a precious 'hour of your *life*'!

Students cannot afford to lose their time in this manner as it will drastically reduce their productivity and make them inefficient in the long run.

The best way to keep track of your time is not by making a mere time table but also by creating a dedicated 'To-Do' list. Even I do that! Once the list is ready, keep on updating it each day, adding useful tasks and deleting useless ones. Life is too short to experiment and then apply!

Always keep that clock behind you for you never know how situations will unfold in future! To understand the significance of time you need nothing but yourself. Observe the modifications time brings in you and around you. Learn to observe nature like a poet for it will act as an anti-stress medication. Often go for nature walks and yes don't consider them as waste of time for they are the fuel that actually accelerates your vehicle.

Talk with your friends only when you have no important task kept in-front of you or left out in your To-Do list!

One essential thing one should keep in mind while setting a target is that the target should be 'just' above your capability. Mind my words...! I said 'just' not simply 'above' because unachievable targets not only demoralise you but also make you lose your valuable energy! Resources much like time are limited and so always be very cautious in spending them.

There are many ways to exploit time. One amongst them is by multitasking, which I won't recommend if you are not that expert. Another way is by talking less and working more. The latter one is better I feel because that is a very proven way of efficient time management. The utilisation of time involves several factors like-

1. Importance of the work you are invested in.

2. Deadline (*most important*)

3. Support from others

4. Number of tasks to accomplish

5. Your work rate

These are the five key factors out of which you can control the last one! Give this a second thought.

Here I hark back to another very important hack to increase productivity by saving time. This is to utilise the 'spaces'. Here spaces refer to the gap or interval between any two major activities. For example, you can plan what you will present in front of the class while traversing from your canteen to your classroom! But don't make crucial decisions in this manner because important decisions in life shape the path to our destiny and therefore while making any important decision, always place your body and mind in a peaceful position for maximum output.

If you don't make use of the spaces you are sure to lose your precious time!

Give preference to your time over anything else! Also learn to value others time or else you will end up being quite selfish which is not at all desirable.

Also never think much about the past events for they are always ready to eat up your present! Also keep aside your future because life will become very dull if you decode your future quite early. The best way to forget these past and upcoming events is by diverting our attention to more important things like reading books, doing exercise, eating healthy etc.

How to Remember Things Faster

Before telling you the trick of remembering faster let me make sure whether you are reading this book with rapt attention or reading is just for the sake of reading. For this I want you to once again recall the factors mentioned in the previous chapter and what was the thing that these factors affected! Now no need to send me the answer by post but just try to analyse your concentration and attention levels!

This is one of the secrets to remembering things faster! If you attend your classes regularly and not only that but also diligently; you will learn things faster. This doesn't mean that merely by attending all the classes and without studying by self you are going to earn colours! But yes if your concentration and attention in class is satisfactory, you will have an upper hand in memorising things faster.

The next secret is to write! Yes I know most of you are already aware of it but I want to give distinct emphasis to writing because that is what I do to remember stuff faster. A key point here to note is that remembering things faster and also forgetting them faster should not happen to you because then that will be like a tumbler with a hole at its bottom. The habit of writing imperative things while studying is a very prudential activity. This also does not mean that you would go on writing anything and everything that comes in front of your eyes. Be very selective because time is always the limiting factor when it comes to writing. Make short notes which are actually short!

Third important secret is by revising again, again and yet again. Although this step is used mostly to retain things, you can use it to remember complex stuff like gigantic flowcharts or very complicated mechanisms.

When you are reading something to remember it keep this point in mind, "I am reading this paragraph so that I can remember it for opportunities may not unfold in the future to read this again."

Don't think stuff like these, "My God! This para is so huge, how am I going to remember it?!", "This is not for me…", "I am sure to forget this para, let me keep it for the night before exam!"

Such sort of discouraging statements will slow down your remembering capability and you will certainly regret later.

How To Retain Things Effectively

If you like to retain things for a longer period of time then let me tell you that there are numerous ways of achieving it. The simplest one is by correlating it with the events or commodities in our daily life or with processes that we are quite familiar with or with already known things. Always try to accept new concepts, theories, activities as top up over already known concepts, theories and activities. And if you bump into something very new, have a deeper study into it and see how it is visible in our daily life or how you can apply it in your life! These things might sound a bit convoluted but then they will help you retain the things for a lengthier duration which will be very supportive in tackling future problems.

Another way of retaining things is by revising them frequently before your brain tends to forget them! This is a very proven method and you can take the benefit of it. Set reminders that you need to revise certain topics from certain subjects and act accordingly. Continuous revision will also reduce the chances of silly mistakes to a greater extent!

Play quizzes with your friends on the topics you find difficult to remember. This will help you get that stuff into your brain in a fun way much like the way we take bitter things along with a sweet substance to nullify their respective effects! You can take the second part of the previous sentence both *literally* as well as *symbolically*!

If you are running out of time then you must opt for this method. Explain the concept that you have extracted by reading the text to either your friend or anyone who is willing to listen to you. Don't hesitate while explaining it to others like a teacher because in that way you will be able to retain at least the explanation part in your memory.

As already mentioned in the previous chapter, writing is a very effective and rational way of retaining things. You must grow a habit of writing things both by looking and without because in your written exams, it is going to help you a lot!

In your school as well as in coaching try to note down the vital things taught in the class. Don't just sit idle listening for you will feel sleepy and most likely doze off!

Taking running notes keeps you alert along with your eyes, ears and most of your body (especially hands). Ask doubts in the class and clear your concepts regarding the topic so that you don't face any issues in the future while revising!

Always go for flow charts and other such sorts of things because they help systematise bulk of text into an effortlessly understandable, presentable as well as learnable entity. Flowcharts are to be used during quick revisions before exams. You can seek help from your teachers while cooking the flow charts if you feel like.

If you forget anything important that you had already studied earlier, don't blame yourself because things will surely be forgotten but just try to give that a second look and make up your mind that from that day onwards you will never forget it again.

Importance of Knowledge

Although most of you know that knowledge is power, very few amongst you actually treat knowledge as power. I am sure that most of you acquire knowledge only to pass your exams and not for…

Not for what? You may ask! See, the process of acquiring knowledge has an irreplaceable characteristic. It gives tremendous pleasure both to the radiator as well as the acquirer. It is therefore said that knowledge should always be shared. Or in other words, knowledge increases on sharing or something like that! When you enjoy the process of acquiring knowledge you will enjoy studying because study imparts us with it. You will no longer become a victim of boredom. Rather you will start developing your unique taste for each subject or each section of a chapter. In this way you will enhance your productivity and you will feel very glad at the end of the sitting. I tested it myself! My friends have also developed interest in this process. When the syllabus is massive only one thing helps and guess what…! It is enjoyment. You will frequently hear people pronouncing that we must enjoy whatever task we perform. Perhaps this is the reason behind them telling so.

Apart from this, knowledge helps you to link yourself with things. It also gives your opinions gravity and it acquires you honour and respect in social circles. Knowledgeable people talk less and listen more! So I request you to do the same. This doesn't at all mean that you will never speak because if you don't speak how will that mere person standing or sitting beside you or in front of you know that you are knowledgeable!

Before going to a debate, a good debater always does plenty of research. He amasses a lot of facts and figures, examples, instances etc. Do you know why? This is because he wants to have a complete knowledge (although not practically possible) about the subject he is advocating for. On the other hand a debater, with little knowledge can't present sufficient evidence and hence loses the game! It is up to you to decide which one you would like to be!

As far as coaching is concerned, it imparts a lot of knowledge. Your duty is to grasp them either by noting them down temporarily in your notebook or permanently in your mind. I would do both! When you share this knowledge with your friends it acts as a revision for you and a passive form of learning for your friend. In this way you can effectively cover a large chunk of your syllabus with comparatively less effort. Give it a try!

How To Score Marks

Perhaps you are a lot more interested in this topic as compared to the previous ones and no worries for I am also anticipating this stage. The answer to this very vibrant question seems to severely vary from mouth to mouth. I was shocked when I encountered this truth for the very first time. For a matter of fact, the pattern of giving marks even varies from teacher to teacher. But as far as objective questions are concerned, this is not the case! Objective questions can be quite scoring if you know the facts but very harsh if you don't!

Some students perform very well in objective questions but fail in subjective tests while the vice versa may be also true! For students of the former category, let me tell you that your brain is very indolent and it doesn't like to mug up long answers while for the second category, your brain is not lethargic but it somewhere lacks in analysing things at depth! Don't get offended for this is what I feel! We can develop ourselves only when we are aware of our weaknesses and so it becomes very critical to spot out the lacunae in ourselves with the help of keen observers! These observers could be your parents, teachers or worthy friends. A true friend will always try to point out your mistakes rather than trying to make you feel good! So always try to respect criticism for criticism helps us develop as complete individuals.

When you make mistakes in your exams don't just say, "Oh no how silly I was…" and put the question paper in your drawer. Rather go through the paper once more with a cool mind and attempt to analyse each and every question. Recollect the approaches that came to your mind during the exam. Try to figure out where and why you got that particular question wrong. Was it because of stress or because you lacked the knowledge! If it was a silly mistake due to stress then figure out the factors which give rise to stress or restlessness in you. This could be time, fear, anxiety, excitement or anything! But if it was because of lack of knowledge then go through that part of the chapter once more. Solve the same problems again and again by altering the values and you will surely benefit.

If you are very weak according to you then let me tell you, you are not alone! The main reasons behind your weakness or inability to score decent marks can be several ranging from distractions like mobile phones, televisions up to the habit of wasting time in futile stuff. Work on these weaknesses and if you are finding it very difficult to handle, take the help of one who has successfully gone through this phase for one who has actually crossed the road knows how to! You should try to become a bit more focused and you should definitely start self-evaluation! After studying every topic, give a test (it could be a self-prepared one). I would hereby like to mention that start employing your time meritoriously and industriously. Become goal oriented alongside maintaining a decent relationship with family and friends. I know this is not that easy but you can do it by minimising your visits to unwanted events or occasions which will provide you some extra time as bonus!

Be regular with your studies. Follow your systematic routine strictly and if required take the guidance of your teachers. Here I would like to share with you a very important tip: Learn your concepts in the class itself. Only keep revisions for home tasks! Utilise your time by compartmenting it according to the subjects you study. The tougher the topic the greater the time you should devote. Don't neglect revisions because they are as important as learning the topic for the first time. Silly mistakes often find home in answer scripts of those who don't revise!

For objective exams, practice thousands of questions and for subjective exams develop the skill of making flow charts and diagrams! Try to structure the answers suitably and underline or highlight the vital phrases in your answer. This trick will draw your examiner's attention and perhaps will provide you fruitful results. Ask your teachers to give feedback on your presentation and expression because at the end of the day, presentation and expressions are the keys that will distinguish your answer from that of your friend! The content and facts in both the answers will be consistent but the way both the answers are structured will vary significantly. Again this is not the case for objective questions as you might know!

After completing your paper, always go through the entire thing once or twice. I did it myself because many a times I knock into words or spellings which I never intended to write. These errors appear quite naturally when there is tremendous pressure on us during the exam in the examination hall. We cannot avoid this pressure but can surely lessen it by-

1. Carrying all necessary stuff along with us while entering the examination hall.

2. Reducing the thinking time

3. Writing answers which are to the point and not beating around the bush.

4. Focusing ourselves in one answer and not thinking about the forthcoming or preceding question.

5. Not thinking about the outcome while writing the exam etc.

How To Balance Coaching With School

Keeping all things apart this is the reason behind you purchasing this book! So in this chapter I will be telling you how to and how not to...!

Firstly 'how to', we know that school is responsible for our holistic growth and development. It teaches us everything including behaviour, conduct, etiquettes, discipline along with manners and academic stuff. We spend most of our dynamic time in schools and so it is our duty to get out some productive results from school. Here I want to tell those students who waste their time in school in futile chit chat that school is a hub of knowledge and you should try your level best to acquire it!

On the other hand, a coaching institute prepares us in an entirely different way. It develops us in a way that we can pierce through a tough resistance to achieve a big dream.

I want you to visualise an inflatable ball. Now school nurtures and increases the radius of the ball while coaching institutes reinforce a particular area of it so that it can face the resistance outside and if required destroy it! Hope you are able to understand.

The combined effect of both school education and that of coaching is a powerful and potential tool everyone should be able to harness. Students who fail to cope up with both of them end up missing a lot of important stuff.

It is fundamentally impossible to give one hundred percent of yourself to both school and coaching at the same time and that is the root of all the problems which you people constantly face. When you align yourself with coaching your grades in school go down and vice versa. Nevertheless let me suggest you some key points or tips that shall help you out in this regard-

1. Don't study the same topic two times i.e. once in school and once in your coaching rather transform one class into revision. Say you were taught a chapter X in your school today and after say three days the same chapter X has been started in your coaching then treat this coaching class as a revision class!

To treat a class as a revision class means to recall the terms and definitions you have already studied along with the progress of the topic. Few people fail to appreciate the importance of revisions. Revisions aid our long term retention and abridges our task of remembering. It adds flavour to the topic and makes it more palatable!

2. Never compromise with the self-study time because it is the backbone of your academic skeleton! Read your textbooks with undeviated concentration and solve numericals with a flexible mindset. Don't try to remember steps or sums. Rather use that ounce of your energy into one or two modest physical exercises during the gap between two study sessions.

3. Make a habit of writing or studying constantly without halt. This is not only going to save your time but will also minimise the chances of getting distracted by unnecessary talks, activities or thinking.

4. Be honest. It is as central as other ethical qualities. Tell your teacher the problems that you face in his/her class and that you are inept to cope up with the school - coaching combination. He/she perhaps will guide you in a better way than any other source.

5. Outline the discrepancies you encounter and clarify them with teachers who understand you.

6. Revisit questions and try to solve them with diverse methods taught in school and coaching. This will make you realise the connection between the two.

7. Feel free to refer to this book anytime whenever you are confused or are in trouble!

In order to survive in times of distress, humans discover a variety of different techniques and tricks. As a student you also have to discover new methodologies of studying so as to minimise the pressure and complete your topics effectively and efficiently. These are some techniques I devised-

1. Write once rather than reading a hundred!

2. Discuss vague concepts with school and coaching friends in between silly talks.

3. Pay a lot of attention in the class and lectures as if trying to grasp up everything taught and carry them forward.

4. Prepare short notes, flow charts and simplified diagrams.

5. Oversimplify concepts (*if you find things very challenging.*)

6. Be regular and punctual. Never miss classes.

7. Be ready with homeworks and assignments.

8. Don't give accommodation to doubts.

9. Revise things before your exam!

10. Revise your answer scripts before submitting.

11. Try to appreciate the concepts and theories designed and developed by great minds because they will make you curious.

12. Develop the appetite for knowledge.

13. Don't relax too much after one exam. Just start preparing for the next. You will get plenty of time to enjoy later on…!

14. Divide and study. It is meaningless to study the same subject the entire day and get bored. Divide your time accordingly and also divide your syllabus in a way you find cooperative.

15. Try your hands on questions after reading and understanding a concept. This is also a phase for application of your knowledge.

16. Obey your parents and teachers.

17. If you get tired then sit in a quiet place and try to self-reflect. Do plenty of yoga and exercise and eat healthy.

18. Stay away from surplus activities and distractions so as to harness the flying time.

How To Analyse Results

Now that you have given your exam and are waiting for your result, try to recreate your mind with hobbies, nature walks, exercise and healthy talks. Go on a trip if you have the time or resources and try to learn something new from it. Bring back memories that you are going to cherish for ages.

Once your results land on your nervous hands go through it yourself. Give it an in-depth reading. Try to figure out your areas of strength and the areas of weakness. Don't compare your results with that of others but with yourself. Start making a strategy based on the available data for your upcoming exam. It could be something like this-

1.   Say this time you prepared two flow charts for each subject. So next time you can upturn this number to four.

2.   Say this time you revised the first chapter three times but didn't read the last chapter even once (say you skipped it). Then next time ensure that you don't have to skip any because of lack of time or anything. And for that to happen, start preparing from now onwards.

3.   Don't waste your time *mugging up*things which could be easily written after understanding the concept properly.

4. Ensure that next time you are going to use a lot of data and examples while writing your answers.

5. For objective questions, solve twice the number of questions you solved this time.

6. Develop a habit of quick revision.

These are only examples and you are free to alter them according to your comfort. You can also add your own points and make a robust strategy out of it. Life is short and there is not much time to experiment with it so always take the help of mock tests to apply and find the result of your strategies. The strategy which fits you the best will get you through this harsh journey.

Importance of Improving Oneself

Lastly before taking adieu I would like to enumerate on the importance of improving oneself. To improve oneself means to raise one's aptitudes and skills to the next level. This can be associated with your personal as well as your professional life. As students you can either improve yourself in your academics or in other co-curricular activities or in both (which is of course not easy). To improve yourself you have to follow certain steps which again can be discovered by oneself. Let me give you one example. Say a boy wants to develop his interpersonal skills. Then the steps he would have to follow are somewhat like this-

1.   He needs to know the complete definition of interpersonal skills.

2.   He needs to get hold of a good book that tells about interpersonal skills.

3.   He needs to read that book with dedication and try to grasp the concepts mentioned there.

4.   He now needs to try the things learnt in real life. For that he can pursue the help of his friends.

5.   After applying the tactics learnt from the book the boy now needs feedback. So he has to hunt for feedback.

6.   If the feedback is positive the boy can now go on and proliferate his skills by attending sessions and seminars.

7. He can also go through a variety of research done in that field and benefit by understanding them.

8. Lastly he now has what he once wanted!

This is only one example for you to understand that nothing is difficult and everything is achievable if you have a strong urge for achieving it. Today's world demands multi-talented individuals who can act as great assets for society. The more the skills you acquire the more will be your worth and more will be your demand in society so my dear friend, go on and get all your pending things completed first and then we will meet each other again in a separate yet new book! See you soon!